just
in
case
you
want
to
fly

julie fogliano

christian robinson

NEAL PORTER BOOKS
HOLIDAY HOUSE / NEW YORK

Neal Porter Books

HOLIDAY HOUSE is registered in the U.S. Patent and Trademark Office.
Printed and bound in March 2019 at Toppan Leefung, DongGuan City, China.
The artwork for this book was made with paint and collage.
Book design by Jennifer Browne
www.holidayhouse.com
First Edition
1   3   5   7   9   10   8   6   4   2

Library of Congress Cataloging-in-Publication Data

Names: Fogliano, Julie, author. | Robinson, Christian, illustrator.
Title: Just in case you want to fly / words by Julie Fogliano ; pictures by Christian Robinson.
Description: First edition. | [New York] : Holiday House, [2019] | "Neal
Porter Books." | Summary: Offers encouragement and supplies, from a snack
and a blanket to a map for finding the way home, to a loved one who may
be facing a new challenge.
Identifiers: LCCN 2018042404 | ISBN 978-0-8234-4344-4 (hardcover)
Subjects: | CYAC: Love—Fiction.
Classification: LCC PZ7.F6763 Jus 2019 | DDC [E]—dc23
LC record available at https://lccn.loc.gov/2018042404

for clio rose,

who fills my bag with just-in-cases

and for all the little birds with big places to go—j.f.

for ben butcher—c.r.

just in case you want to fly
here's some wind

and here's the sky

here's a feather
here's up high

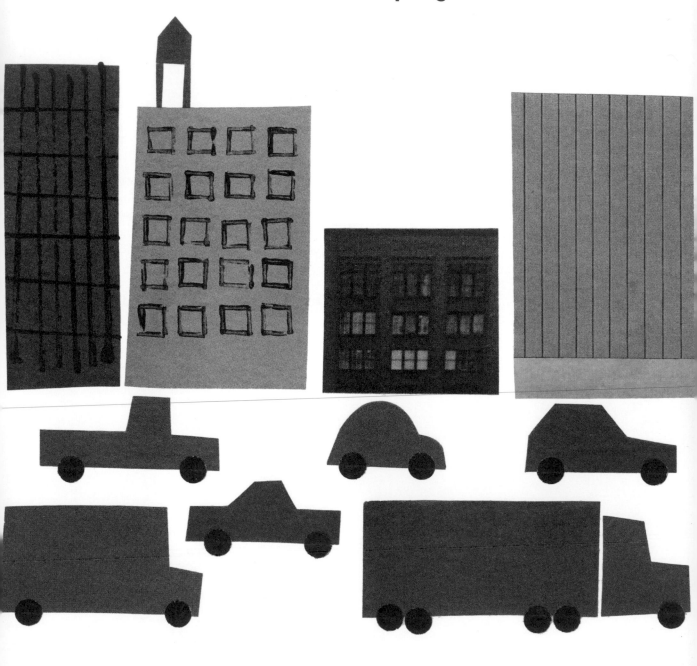

and here's a wing
from a butterfly

here's a cherry  if you need a snack

and if you get itchy
here's a scratch on the back

here's a rock to skip

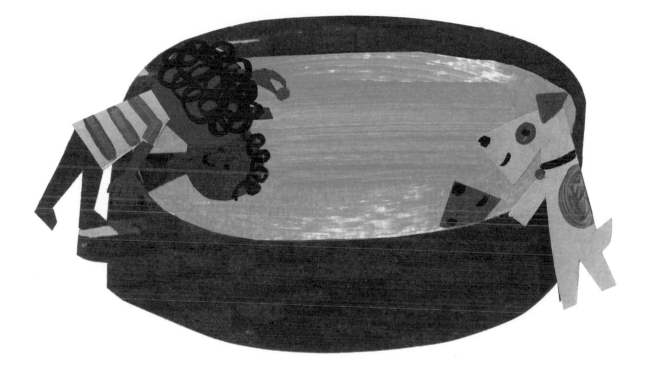

and a coin to wish

and a fork

and a spoon

and a cup

and a dish

and just in case you want to sing
here's a la la la

and a

ding
ding
ding

here's a joke
if you want to laugh

and here's your
toothbrush

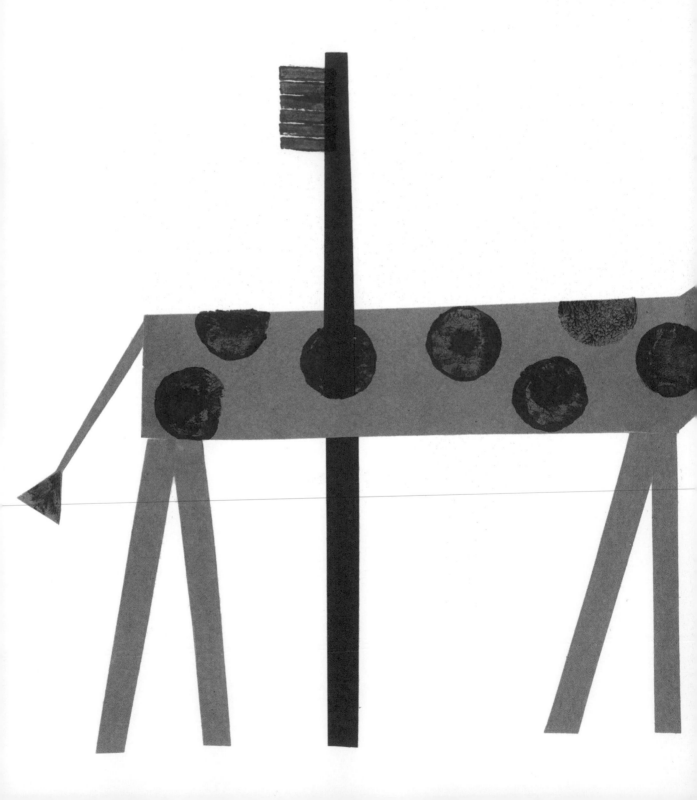

and your
favorite
giraffe

here's a blanket

and here's a dream

and some kisses
on your head

here's a pillow

and here's a song
for when you go to bed

and just in case you want to cry
here is a tissue
and here's a sigh

here's an umbrella
in case it rains

and some honey for your tea

and here is a map
with an x on the spot
to find your way
home to me